IF WISHES
WERE HORSES

ANNE MCCAFFREY

IF WISHES WERE HORSES

A ROC BOOK

ROC
Published by the Penguin Group
Penguin Putnam Inc., 375 Hudson Street, New York, New York 10014, U.S.A.
Penguin Books Ltd, 27 Wrights Lane, London W8 5TZ, England
Penguin Books Australia Ltd, Ringwood, Victoria, Australia
Penguin Books Canada Ltd, 10 Alcorn Avenue, Toronto, Ontario, Canada M4V 3B2
Penguin Books (N.Z.) Ltd, 182–190 Wairau Road, Auckland 10, New Zealand

Penguin Books Ltd, Registered Offices: Harmondsworth, Middlesex, England

First published by Roc, an imprint of Dutton NAL,
a member of Penguin Putnam Inc.

First Printing, October, 1998
10   9   8   7   6   5   4   3   2   1

Copyright © Anne McCaffrey, 1998

RoC REGISTERED TRADEMARK—MARCA REGISTRADA

LIBRARY OF CONGRESS CATALOGING-IN-PUBLICATION DATA:
McCaffrey, Anne.
If wishes were horses / Anne McCaffrey.
p.   cm.
ISBN 0-451-45642-4 (alk. paper)
I. Title.
PS3563.A255I35   1998
813'.54—dc21   98-23917
                                                   CIP

Printed in the United States of America
Set in Goudy
Designed by Julian Hamer

This book is printed on acid-free paper. ∞

IF WISHES
WERE HORSES

OF COURSE, MANY PEOPLE in our small county village sought advice and help from my mother long before the War started because she was quite wise as well as gifted with a healing touch. Often, day and night, we would hear the front door knocker—shaped like a wyvern it was, with a stout curled tail—bang against the brass sounding circle. That summons was undeniable, echoing through the Great Hall and up the stairs. There was no sleeping once someone started pounding. Sometimes they didn't pound but tapped, quietly but insistently, so that one was awakened more by the muted repetition than the noise. From the time I was twelve, I got roused quite as often as my mother did. Of course, I was also able to turn over and go back to sleep, which my mother could not.

"Those of us who *can* help *should not* deny it to others," my mother was apt to say, usually to still my father's grumblings. "I'll just see what I can do for them."

"Day *and* night?" my father would demand in an exasperated or frustrated tone of voice.

However, he was such a heavy sleeper that he was rarely disturbed when she slipped from the huge oak fourposter bed to answer the summons. As I grew older and she began to rely on me to assist her from time to time, I realized that he never answered the nocturnal rapping, though occasionally Mother would send me to wake him to help us. What I never did figure out—then—was how she knew, on our way down the main staircase, that she would *need* his protection to answer that particular summons.

"Oh, it's nothing mysterious, Tirza love," Mother told me. "If you listen, you'll learn quick enough the difference in the *sound* of the knocking. That can tell me a lot."

It took me nearly two years before I could differentiate between the hysterical, the urgent, or the merely anxious kind of rapping.

Mother's ability to have some sort of a solution to almost any problem had become somewhat legendary in our part of the Principality. She had a fund of general knowledge, an unfailing sympathy augmented by common sense, and a remarkable healing touch.

"Much of the time, Tirza, they only need someone who *listens*, and they end up knowing their *own* solutions. You may well have inherited the family failing, love," she went on with a sigh. When she saw my stunned expression, she had added cheerfully, "But we won't know that for a while yet. Oh, it could be worse, know. You could have inherited Aunt Simona's teeth."

That was quite enough to send me into the giggles.

"Oh, I am terrible!" And she rolled her eyes in mock-penitence. "However could I be so unkind as to mention Aunt Simona's teeth! I may have no jam with tea tonight." Her lovely eyes twinkled. "Now do be a *good* child and get me some clean bottles for this lotion I've just made for Mistress Chandler."

Nonetheless, I never heard anyone, not even Father, refer to Mother's ministrations as failings. Except perhaps Aunt Simona, who had more than large, protruding front teeth to make her unlovable. Mother also had an unerring ability to know who was speaking from the heart, telling the truth, and who might be unwilling to own up to the consequences of his or her actions. Father would invariably delay his magisterial sittings until she could join him, though her participation was confined to sitting quietly at one end of the table. Strangers would try to prevaricate or settle blame elsewhere, but she was never deceived in any particular. She and Father must have worked out some sort of private signals, for she never spoke at these sessions, merely listened. Father was the one who pounced on the culprit and would be in possession of details that would stun the miscreant, often into a terrified and more accurate account of what had happened. So, if Lady Talarrie Eircelly was known for her wisdom and healing, Lord Emkay Eircelly was equally renowned for fair and firm justice.

During the day, village women were more apt to come to the kitchen door, slipping into the big warm room with all its marvelous aromas and giving Livvy some hint of what their problem was. A cup of tea and a "morsel to eat with it"—anything from a slab of cake or plate of fresh sweet biscuits—would be instantly served by our Livvy. Even if that had not been Mother's standing order, Livvy was the sort of person who knew the soothing properties of nice hot tea and a treat or two. Some folk eased in quietly, almost apologetically; others would already be in tears and found themselves comforted by Livvy's ample self. The shyer men would come to the kitchen, too, murmuring about not wishing to disturb her ladyship.

"Which same," Livvy would say tartly when she sent Tess to guide them to wherever Mother was at that time of day, "is exactly what they want to do and why they came. Mostly," Livvy added, banging her pots and lids about or doubling the energy with which she did her present task, "all they need is to hear pure common sense. If they'd stop and *think*, which a body should be able to do, they'd see how to handle things. Seems to me as if they have to have Authority give 'em the word. Wear Milady out, so they will." This threat would be accompanied by one of her gusty sighs. "And that's not fair on her. What'll happen if they've wore her out so much she's unable to see to all the things she has to do in any one day or another?"

"Could they wear Mother out?" my brother, Tracell, asked, startled. We had seen the latest arrival, for he had skulked about the herb garden, getting up the courage to come to the kitchen door. And we, dreadful children that we were, had followed—just in case there might be something we could wheedle out of Livvy when she had finished dispensing hospitality to him. "I heard her tell Aunt Rachella that it was having babies that wears her out."

"Most it would, the way she has them," Livvy had said with a snort. "Two at a time."

"Catron came by herself," Tracell reminded her.

Livvy humphed. "Well-bred ladies like your dear mother ought not to be having twins. That's for common folk, not *ladies!*"

"Why not?"

"Now, Lady Tirza, that's not for me to tell you and you

6

will kindly forget . . . what was just said. I wouldn't want anyone saying I'd said a word against Lady Talarrie." And she passed us the plate of lady cakes.

"Mother's not having another set of twins, is she?" Tracell demanded anxiously.

"I should hope not!" Livvy said so firmly that we knew she must, indeed, know.

Anyway, Mother had always told us, her oldest, when new babies were coming. She'd even known that Catron was coming by herself. Then she had Andras and Achill. And, when Father came back from the Miriseng Campaign, she told us that the next pair would be girls, Diana and Desma.

"So, don't you fret, young Tracell," Livvy said, putting the now empty plate in the sink, "about your lady mother. She's got strength for seven and sense for a dozen. Just do your best not to add to the trials and tribulations everyone else brings her."

"She's *our* mother," Tracell said stoutly.

"For which you should be eternally grateful. Now out of my kitchen! I can hear her ladyship's step, and you've

7

no need to be here to embarrass young Sten. Like as not, she'll have to bring him through here to the still room, so make yourselves scarce."

As we could hear my mother's voice with the phrase that ever seemed to be on her lips, "I'll just see what I can do about that right now . . ." we were out the door in a flash.

"I'll see what I can do about it," was Mother's habitual response to most matters brought to her attention.

In itself, the phrase was unusually effective. For instance, the day Tray fell off his pony and broke one of the bones in his forearm, her calmly confident, "Now I'll just see what I can do about this . . ." cut him off mid-howl even though she had just given a careful yank on his wrist. I had heard the grate of the bones as they settled into line again. We used our two riding crops as temporary splints, tied on with the flounce of Mother's petticoat. Tray was too surprised and—I must say—rather brave to forego any further outcry, though he was dreadfully pale until we got him back to the house and into his bed.

* * *

I'm not sure why bad news has to pick nice, sunny spring days to arrive and alter perfectly contented lives. But I had noticed that Mother had been wearing all three of her special crystals for the last few days, and usually she wore only the one. She had also been casting frequent glances up the north road, outside the gates of Mallafret Hall that led to Princestown. I did too, having caught her nervousness, but it was she in the end who saw the messenger, beating his lathered and weary horse up the long drive. Immediately she summoned my father from his study, sent me to get ale, bread and cheese from the kitchen, and ordered Tray to collect one of our fast and durable hunters from the stables.

"Bring up that bright bay, the one you say has no bottom to him," she said. "Bridled."

"No saddle?"

"The messenger will use his own."

"What messenger?" asked Tray, because the thick trunks of the oak trees that lined the drive briefly masked the oncoming rider.

"The one on his way up the avenue. Go! Now!"

No one argued with that tone in Mother's voice, and

9

Tray raced for the stables as I ran to the kitchen. So we all appeared, along with Father, just as Prince Sundimin's courier, his face gaunt with fatigue, as exhausted as the lathered mount who staggered up our drive, reached the wide front stairs.

His message, while brief, was momentous, announcing that Prince Refferns of Effester had started a war with our Principality. Our good Prince Sundimin perforce had to raise an army to defend our cities and lands. All liegemen were to honor their oath to their prince.

"Lord Eircelly," the herald gasped, "muster your men with all possible speed." Then he blinked with gratitude at the tankard of ale, which I held up to him while Mother gestured he should moisten his dry throat before continuing. "Deepest thanks, milady. Milord, the prince bade me to deliver into your very hands this message," and he handed over a square of parchment, "and to assure you that the matter is of the gravest urgency." He then tipped the tankard, drinking a good half of its contents. "I must also beg the favor of a replacement mount, milord," he continued, "since I have far yet to go before I finish my assigned task." Stiffly, he swung his right leg over the cantle and would have fallen against the horse had not my father, leaping forward, immediately lent a hand to steady him.

"The favor is already granted, I see," my father said at his driest, with a glance at Tray, who was leading a bright bay from the stable yard.

"Sit, sir, and eat while we change the saddle," Mother said and all but pushed the messenger onto the broad wing of the shallow stairs of Mallafret Hall.

"Very good, my thanks, milady, milord. I was urged not to stop . . ."

"Changing horses is scarcely a stop, my man," my father said, "and you must restore yourself or you'll not go much further on. Have you to ride all the way to the sea?"

The weary man nodded, his mouth too full of bread and cheese to speak.

"The road is good, the way is clear, and the sunshine will hold," Mother said.

By then, Tray and Father had changed the saddle to

the bay's back. As the man made two attempts to swing aboard his fresh mount, Mother tucked a second loaf in the saddlebag and urged him to eat as he rode onward.

"The bay is genuine," Father said. "Trust him. God's speed!"

Father stepped back and the man immediately kneed his fresh horse into a canter. He gave one wave as he turned right at the gate toward his next stop and the distant sea.

"For that matter," Tray said, "he could probably sleep on the bay and he'd keep going until he's reined in. And you, my brave lad?" Tray asked the splay-legged, drooping headed mount whose breath came in wheezing gasps. "Shall we save you?"

Father looked up from breaking the seal of the message with all its dangling official princely stamps.

"I shan't expect the impossible, Tracell," my father said, gently, "but I'd hazard that he's one of those marvelous plains' Cirgassians and worth the effort."

"A Cirgassian?" Tray exclaimed, really looking at the exhausted animal.

"Just look at the ears, the fine head, the deep barrel . . .

12

if we can save him, we should try. Do see what you can do." Then, having broken the seals, his eyes flicked through the usual florid opening paragraphs to the important part of how many men he must bring in answer to this muster.

"Last year's bad season in Effester has made Prince Refferns envious of our prosperity?" my mother asked.

"As you so often do, my dear Talarrie, you have hit upon the crux of the matter. We are enjoined to give our liege prince the service and support due him as quickly as is humanly possible."

"Then the Shupp is low from the drought?" Mother asked.

"Correct as usual, my prescient love. Tracell, see this poor fellow stabled in the thickest bed of straw you and Surgey can make, and groom him into such comfort as he may enjoy in his sad condition. Or would you rather take the drum to the village and announce the muster?"

To my brother's credit, the care of a horse of such a distinguished breed ranked first in importance. So it fell to Sir Minshall as Seneschal, with young Emond beating the drum, to speed to the village square to announce an

13

immediate muster and set the disaster bell to pealing out its summons. There were plenty of young lads in the village to send to apprise outlying farms, beyond the range of even that melodious bell, of the emergency and the haste that must be made in answer to the summons. Mother, Livvy, and I helped Father pack his saddlebags, add an almost unneeded burnish to his armor, for Emond was not careless with his duties as equerry, and roll up his travel blankets and gear.

Father immediately dispatched an advance party of armed troopers and appointed dawn by the next morning as the moment of departure for the larger force. Thirty mounted knights there were, plus fifty foot soldiers, the muster that our prince required of my father from his oath of fealty. Father looked very pleased with the speed at which all had assembled, ready to travel. More was in readiness than could have been expected for all it had been decades since the prince had had to call upon his liegemen to defend his borders.

"Scarce twenty hours between the call to arms and our response," Father murmured to my mother and me, for Tracell now held the bridle of Father's heavy-boned war steed in the courtyard. In the courtyard and spilling beyond the graveled avenue, digging up the lawn with heavy boots and shod hooves, were the others, banners unfurled and faces grim.

"Speed is surely a requirement in any muster," my mother said proudly and lifted her face for his farewell kiss.

"I didn't think to assemble so smartly, though," my father said, holding her in his arms.

"I am not the only competent one in this Hall," she said in an attempt at levity.

Did I see tears in my father's eyes at this moment of farewell? Possibly mine were overfull as well for I was frightened. All the soldiery looked so brave in their fine uniforms, all the metal shiny and dangerous.

Everyone who could have come to see our brave men depart, lining the avenue where they could, and the northern road as far as we could see.

"I can leave all else in your hands, my dear Competence," my father said to my mother as he stamped his feet into his heavy boots, the ones with extra flaps above the knee to prevent sword cuts to his thighs. The other armsmen of Mallafret Hall were no less efficient in

15

preparing themselves and had organized baggage wains, pack animals, ammunition and additional horses.

"Had you a warning you kept to yourself, Talarrie?" I heard my father softly ask my mother though they did not know I was within hearing distance.

Mother's hand went unerringly to the crystals she wore on the long chains about her neck.

"I'd knowledge of a sort, so I thought to have everyone check their equipment. We can also be thankful that the year gave us a good spring to plant in."

"My wise and lovely Talarrie," and there was a pause as they clung together.

"You will be safe, my love," she added as she stepped back, fingers tight about the crystals.

So the troop moved at a smart trot, the foot soldiers hanging on to stirrup leathers to keep up with the mounted troops. They were cheered out of the gates of the Hall, and relatives and friends fell in behind the troop, accompanying them well up the main road to Princestown. With unbecoming pride, I hoped that they would be first to join the main army of Prince Sundimin.

"When will they come back, Mother?" I asked when

16

our brave troop was so far away that we could no longer see the dust the horses kicked up. I had been very much aware of the sorrow in my mother's eyes and the tense grip of her fine fingers on her crystals.

"Not soon enough, Tirza," Mother said with a sad little smile. "And not all who left here this morning." Then she gave me a little smile, cupping my head in her hand. "But *he* will return." She released the crystals, picked up her skirts, and went back into the house.

"Surely the war won't take long, will it, Mother?" asked my brother. After the scurry to get everyone prepared, he looked disgruntled. At fourteen he was much too young to be mustered with the men and, as my father's heir, he could not even go as drummer as had fourteen-year-old Riaret, the smith's lad. Tray adored our father, as indeed he should, and while some of his lessons included the studying of old battles and sieges and such like, he certainly ought to have known that wars had a habit of taking far longer than the most optimistic opinion. But then, Father always won the mock-engagements they invented in three days, four at most.

I knew before my mother answered that the war would

not be short or a four-day rout: one of those awful premonitions to which I was prone. I tried very hard not to let them insert themselves in my mind, but they appeared as they chose. Like waking one morning, when I was ten, and knowing that Father's best stallion had impaled himself on a stake in the top field and bled to death. Or knowing that my youngest sister, Desma, was choking on a pea that had fallen out of her rattle. But Mother had known, too, and reached her in time to scoop out the impediment and open the path of air to her lungs.

"The war will take whatever time is required to end it," Mother told Tray, which was not the answer he wanted. "Do close your mouth, Tray. You wouldn't want to swallow a fly."

I also knew what else worried my twin, but then we were closely bonded in our twinship. My father had promised Tracell the pick of the young horses for his sixteenth birthday, one that he could train on his own. Right now our fields and stables were virtually empty of all but brood mares and the one stallion too old for battle. And the foundered Cirgassian.

"If the war lasts very long, there won't be a horse for me on my sixteenth birthday," Tracell complained as we followed Mother inside Mallafret Hall.

"If that should be the case," Mother said cheerfully, "I'll be sure to do something about it, my love. You *will* have the promised steed on your birthday. I'll see to that."

That was reassurance enough for Tracell, who lost his worried frown and quite pranced.

"Of course," Mother went on with a sly glance at him, "you must now share with me many of the duties your father undertakes, for I shall need a strong man at my side during the times to come."

"But Sir Minshall is Seneschal," my brother said.

"And he is very well known to have been a fine soldier, winning many battles . . . in his day," my mother replied. "He will look finely fierce if I am required to give audience to men of rank, but it is on you whom I rely: you and Tirza."

"Yes, of course, Mother," we said in chorus.

*   *   *

So that was one reason that I *knew* that we were in for a long separation from Father, which increased my original foreboding.

I said nothing but clasped Mother's hand tightly when hers closed on mine. So she knew that I knew and was warning me not to speak. Unlike Tracell, who speaks without thought most of the time, I somehow have the sense to know when to keep silent. Of course, with such a collection of brothers and sisters all demanding attention, I had little opportunity to get words in edgewise. Tracell had always talked for the pair of us, even when we were learning to speak and I had been content to let him. Until the time I heard Nurse fretting to my mother that she worried that I talked so seldom.

"Ah, but when she does speak, she speaks in good sentences and to a purpose," my mother had said, stroking my hair and hugging me. "My gracious silence," she added, smiling at me and her smiles were worth all the words in the world.

"If you say so, milady," my nurse had replied, still dubious.

After that, I made an effort to talk, though sometimes

20

the only things to be said were so obvious that it was almost a waste of breath to mention them. Why comment on the obvious? Like a sunny day. Or a good soaking rain to encourage crops and flowers to grow. Or how well the youngest twins were doing.

By the time I was twelve, I learned that some people would say one thing—as often my father's tenants did—and yet you could hear what they should have said, or wanted to say and didn't dare. There were times when I knew I should mention the disparity to Father or Mother. Sometimes I did not. Unless, of course, Mother took me to one side and asked, "What does my gracious silence think?" Which meant it was proper for me to speak out.

Unlike Tracell's anxiety to be given a fine horse for his sixteenth birthday, I had always known that the present that would be mine when I became sixteen was safely in Mother's locked chest, hidden behind the fireplace in her room. I *knew* that the crystal had been there since my birth, for it was a distaff tradition that crystals were given to each daughter on the occasion of her sixteenth birthday. Even the ones for my other sisters—Catron, Diana and Desma—were safely in keeping. (Mother had known the outcome of each of her pregnancies: that my next youngest sister, Catron, would arrive by herself. Followed by two more boys, Andras and Achill, then Diana and Desma.)

The rest of that auspicious day when Father answered the call of his prince was odd for we were both elated at how quickly the muster had been made and then suddenly bereft of important tasks to be done. I did help Tray with the Cirgassian. He had the most delicate pointy ears—still drooping in his exhaustion. He would need much care if he were to survive.

"I've never seen a Cirgassian before," Tray remarked to Surgey as they gently groomed the last of the hardened lather and dirt from its flanks. It stood, head down in the stable, golden straw up to its belly. Tray would offer it water from time to time but kept the portions small.

"Worth our effort, sor," Surgey agreed.

"Maybe you'll cure him well enough to be ridden again," I suggested, though I wasn't all that sure of it. It would be very good for Tray if the animal recovered.

For my brother was much too long in the leg anymore for his pony.

"Well, I shall certainly see what I can do about this fellow," Tray said, hands on his hips,. He sounded so like Mother that I stared at him until he was aware of my astonishment and gave me a grin. "After all, Mother only does what needs to be done and I know what needs to be done with him."

Which was, of course, the exact and complete truth, and so I was quite as happy to help my twin as I would be to assist Mother.

Of course, as messages began to arrive from the battle lines, there was much more to think about. Father's troops had responded so expeditiously that they shamed the musters of other villages on the way into doubling their efforts to swell the ranks at Princestown. And thus our Prince Sundimin was able to meet the initial attack of the aggressor, Prince Refferns of Effester. That prince, thinking to find an easy mark in our Principality, did not. In fact, he was pushed back across the River Shupp, which was the boundary between our Principalities. If my father's messages to us singled out the most valiant of our townsmen, and those whose bravery had cost them their lives, the messages the heralds proclaimed suggested that our father's leadership had been the primary cause of our success. Prince Sundimin was an older, cautious man who had not previously had to take up arms to defend his borders. I could see that the "games" my father had played with Tracell and those he had inveigled into their maneuvers had been far more beneficial than many such other pastimes.

But the war dragged on because, Prince Refferns, deprived of an easy victory, employed mercenaries to strengthen his weakened lines, certain from the ease and force with which his army had been beaten back across the Shupp, that Sundimin would press the advantage. So, perforce, Sundimin had to make alliances with other Princedoms, west and south of our Principality to be sure that Effester, now advised by professional soldiers, did not outflank him.

"We can see them across the wide river," Father wrote Mother—she always read his infrequent letters to us (though perhaps not every word he wrote) "and they us, but there isn't a bridge left now for many leagues on either side of the Shupp. All have been burned so do not look for the usual supplies from the east. Be sure to gather in the harvest and preserve it well."

Mother had not needed that advice. The day after Father and his company had left, she had distressed Siggie the head gardener to the point of tears when she made him dig up all the flowers—save for the roses—and plant vegetables, using the arbors for beans, tomatoes, squash and peas. She sent word to all our villagers that they were to do likewise, and had the gamekeepers increase the snares for rabbit and coney, and for pheasant and grouse, and culled the deer of the old or lame which would have been allowed to die as their time came. She had us all out in the ornamental lakes of the formal gardens, deepening the long rectangles so that we, like the farmers, could stock pond waters with river tench, bream and carp. The wood lakes received her attention as well, and the forest streams so that we had racks and racks of drying fish while the cooper's apprentices were increased to twenty as the orders for kegs, barrels and tuns came in. I have never spent such a busy summer but somehow Mother had the knack of making the work seem both novel and one more way of keeping Father and all our friends in his company well supplied when winter came.

At harvest time, while the battles seemed to seesaw across the Shupp by way of pontoon bridges or other craft tied together, even the oldest villagers were put to work, sitting down if they could not stand or glean, or perched on high stools to flail the seed from the full heads of the crop. She had the hedgerows scoured for useful herbs, which were dried against need. And because we children worked beside her and the villagers, no complaint came to our ears as we worked all the long summer hours God gives a day in our latitude.

"Sure'n' we could feed all Prince Sundimin's armies with what we've here," someone remarked.

"Sure'n what else are we doing this for?" was the doughty response.

So it surprised no one when my father sent a letter asking for what supplies could be spared, for the armies were wintering along the river Shupp, neither force willing to withdraw. And more princelings, further down the river,

26

all the way to the seaport, began to eye each other across the broad Shupp. Since Mallafret had huge, dry cellars, much had been stored with us as well as in the three great village barns. The last of our horses pulled the wagons. Our farmers themselves accompanied the drays pulled by their oxen, determined to return with the beasts no matter what. They managed, but only because Father sent an escort along with them to be sure of their return. And because meat—even haunches of our venison—had been part of our offerings, the oxen did not have to be sacrificed.

In one exception, Mother had also had us older five children secrete a portion—a tithe, she called it—in the deepest and darkest cellars of Mallafret where few would look for anything other than seemingly blank walls. And she enjoined us to secrecy.

"You mean the war is going on and on, don't you, Mother?" Tracell said gloomily, for we were both now fifteen.

"I said I'd see what I can do about your birthday horse, Tracell," she said firmly.

"Mother, you're as clever as you can stare," Tray said

with a certain maturity in his voice—for his voice was now a firm tenor, "but with so many horses needed by the army, however will there be one for me? Besides Courier who can barely walk without wheezing." For that was what we had named the Cirgassian who had somehow survived his ordeal.

"I intend to see what I can do." And she walked off on some other of the many duties that were her never-ending responsibility in Father's absence.

"Tray, I could kick you," I said, keeping my voice low but meaning him harm, "to doubt Mother so."

He gave me a long look. "I have every respect for our mother, Tirza, but there are some things even she will find it difficult to provide in these times."

The unmistakable sound of cannon and the discharge of other weapons wakened us one cold wintry morning just before Solstice. While rousing the rest of us to close and bar the shutters of the all-too-many windows of Mallafret Hall, Mother sent Tray to see what had happened and to offer shelter to the villagers. The barrage was at least sporadic and the Shupp, half a mile beyond the village, was full of wintry snow and rain, running too rapidly to allow ice to form—and thus preventing easy access from our enemy. Tray, hauling his long legs up almost to his chin, galloped bareback off on the pony, who was speedier of foot than the poor wind-broken Courier.

"While he's gone, we must see what we can do to protect ourselves should the enemy somehow cross the river and seek to pillage," Mother said and briskly gave her orders.

"But what *can* we do, milady?" Sir Minshall demanded, for Mallafret was a manor house, not a castle, though it was stoutly built of the native golden stone.

"Sir Minshall, we may be women and young folk, but there is much that we all can do. And will!" she said so staunchly that he blushed with shame. "We have lances, we have the old long rifles—and powder and shot for them, if I am not mistaken. We have crossbows and quarrels from an even earlier war, and bows and arrows even now used to hunt deer. We have heights from which we can pour boiling oil on those who might seek to enter

Mallafret. First, girls, go shutter every window. Sir Minshall, Surgey, Siggie, be so good as to pull the heaviest chests across the doorways. Livvy, Tess, Tirza, take our largest kettles and boil oil. Not the new pressings. The old will do as well, and be sure to have lighted torches so we give them a good roasting once they've been soaked in oil."

"We have so many doors, milady," Sir Minshall said anxiously.

"And quite likely as many nails. Fetch the stout planks we use to clean the ceilings and refresh the chandeliers. I'll see what else I can do."

When I helped carry the first of the cauldrons up the many flights of stairs to be settled just over the main entrance, I could see that the village was afire. Leaving Tess and Livvy to arrange the "welcome" blessing of hot oil, I raced to tell Mother.

"Tray will know to bring the survivors back to us. Let us devoutly hope some have weapons," she said. "Stuff my lavender scarf through the shutters above the secret door, for that is the only one unsealed. Tray will have sense enough to see what is meant by it."

"No one can have used it in hundreds of years," I said, for although we of the Eircellys knew of its existence, not even Tray or I would have dared use it—for fear someone might oversee us.

Mother favored me with a smile. "Not used, to be sure, but kept oiled and passable. One never does know when something like that will be needed."

Somehow that forethought of hers turned my fear to resolution. Whatever we must do to secure Mallafret from pillage and destruction *would* be done and be sufficient to our need.

Tray did return, four small children sitting numbly on his pony, and behind him, carrying what they had been able to save, walked many of the village women. Luckily the pony fit through the secret door, though first the children had to be taken from his back.

"The men have all stayed to defend what homes remain," Tray said, his face covered with smuts and one hand blistered. He also carried a musket someone had supplied him. "But Effestrians cannot cross," he added fiercely. "Not that they didn't try, but they did not take into account the current and have been carried so far below us, toward the first rapids, that I doubt they will survive the journey or make another attempt. Farms are sending reinforcements to assist us, so I shall return now, having discharged my duty to our people."

"Only after I have seen what I can do about your hand, my son," my mother said proudly and shortly attended his injury. As he left, taking the pony with him out the secret door, I saw her hand clutching the crystals. She saw my gaze on her action and nodded solemnly. "He will be all right," she murmured before she drew me back to help her attend others. "Now let us see what we can do to settle these people."

"Yes, Mother," I said, following.

"Who is hurt?" she called in a voice that could be heard across the Great Hall, now filled with weeping and fretting folk. "Tirza, we will need hot water and tea, and perhaps a tot of something stronger to restore spirits."

"Let us do that, milady," the cooper's wife said, stepping forward. She had served at the hall before her marriage and knew where things were kept.

"That is an excellent thought, Merva," Mother said, "much appreciated. Tirza, if you will separate the injured from the sound, then we can continue with our preparations to defend Mallafret."

"I doubt they would be able to come ashore, milady," Merva said stoutly. "Not only is the current swift but the river itsel' is filled with ... things ... that bump and slither and can easily overturn the silly rafts they made. An' as soon as the first cannon went, so my man took the last horse with four good legs and rode to summon such as are left to come to our aid."

"Well done, but Quiman has always been sensible," my mother said approvingly and Merva preened before she recalled herself to the tasks at hand.

With all the heavy cauldrons full of hot oil, every other pan of size in the kitchen had to be used to cook a morning porridge while other women continued with the bread which Livvy had set to rise. By the time all stomachs were full of a warm and nourishing meal, Mother had a good idea of the destruction wrecked on the village from talking to those as she served them. Only two of the cannon balls had landed on targets, yet so many cottages had been built butt-on-butt that almost the whole river-side row, including the inn, the school, and the church had burned. That left over a hundred and fifty without shelter and deprived of most of their belongings—beds and clothes being the most critical of the losses in this depth of winter. And the Solstice but a week away. Handcrafts made for the celebration, new clothing, and other gifts as well as foodstuffs hoarded for a good feasting were likewise so much ash.

"I'll have to see what I can do," Mother said, fingering her crystals, and I did wonder how she would manage to rise to this disaster. Especially with Mallafret not yet secure from attack.

Midafternoon a troop raced up the avenue led by sons of nearby estates, too young yet to be mustered—although if the war continued much longer, they too would be called up. Tray, of course, rode in the lead, proudly astride his pony, his legs stuck out in front of him so they wouldn't drag on the ground.

Although the sight of Tray reassured both Mother and

me, we nevertheless greeted the new arrivals with such men as we had left and three of the largest women. Sir Minshall had been unable to stoop sufficiently to use the secret door, but he manned one of the long rifles bristling through the slits of the shutters.

"The Effestrian force perished at the rapids, Mother," Tray said, dismounting by the expedient of standing up on his long legs and letting the pony walk out from under him. His face was filthy and he had scrapes on his face and arms where the sleeves were torn, but his blistered hand was still protected by a very dirty bandage. "I've left pickets both north and south," and he pointed, "and we met a scouting party from Princestown who came to see how far south the Effestrians managed to push. We are advised that Prince Monteros is moving his forces north as fast as he can. Though some say," and now Tray sounded quite cynical, "that he is not apt to pursue anyone past his own borders." He had been moving towards her as he spoke and now embraced her. "It's all right now, Mother. Mallafret is safe."

"And you will be hungry, no doubt," Mother said

smiling as if he had been on an outing with friends. "We can certainly do something about that!"

Tray waved his good hand diffidently. "If you will pack it up for us, please. We will quarter ourselves in the village to be sure the enemy does not return, seeking the cannon which we caused to fall into the Shupp."

"Oh!"

I believe that was the first time I ever saw my mother at a complete loss for words. Then she gripped Tray by the arms, her face beaming with pride. "So it wasn't running that pony through the woods that caused you so many scratches?"

"Indeed not, milady," said the scion of another family, grinning from ear to ear. "Thought Tray's plan a capital one, since most of us know the ways of our river and how to cross safely. I am Keffine, son of Lord Hyland." He gave as courtly a flourish as if he had been clad in silks instead of torn and soot-smutted leathers.

"How are you for ammunition?" Mother asked.

"Sufficient, milady," Keffine said, tapping bulky saddle-bags.

"Much of the village is burned," she added.

"We'll fare well, milady," the scion said and jerked his head at Tray. "We must settle in for the night and set our watches."

"All are safe here?" Tray asked, looking at the tightly boarded house.

"We shall be quite safe." My mother kissed his cheek, a maternal salute that he bore with considerably more poise than he would once have managed.

The pony had come back to stand beside him, and swinging his leg wide and across the little beast, Tray reined him about and led his tatterdemalion troop back down the avenue.

"He deserves a proper horse," I heard my mother mutter as we made our way back to the secret door—scarcely a secret now, but useful with every other entrance to the house barricaded. "I shall just have to see what I can do about that."

"We've more than a year till we're sixteen, mother," I said.

"I know." Within that sad acknowledgement was her

unspoken knowledge that this was not likely to end before the sixteenth anniversary of our birth. I felt almost guilty that I would wear my crystal but Tracell, who had shown such mature fortitude and intelligence, would be disappointed.

While Mallafret Hall had over twenty bedchambers, it did not have sufficient warm coverings for so many unexpected guests. Even bringing all the horse rugs in from the stable did not suffice and, for the second time in a single day, I saw my mother thwarted in her incredible ability to cope with any crisis, disaster or problem.

"I shall have to do *something*," I heard her murmur, clutching her crystals and furiously rubbing them, forcing them to provide an answer.

"Mother, is it possible there're some usable things stored in the presses and trunks in the attics?" All of us children had played up there on rainy days.

"Ooh, milady," Tess said, brightly, "there's ever so many things up there. We had to turn out all the old curtains and things before Lord Emkay left."

Mother's face lit up. She was so delighted that she hugged us both indiscriminately.

"The very things indeed. All those dreary, dreary tapestries that I couldn't bear to throw out! They shall do admirably."

If there was a slight musty smell from being stored so long, no one minded for the heavy brocaded draperies as well as the tapestries were good insulation against the cold. And all, even the rugs that were also discovered in at the apex of roof and rafter, had been carefully wrapped against the moth and provided covering for even the flagstones of the Great Hall. With fires in every hearth, everyone would be able to sleep with more comfort than they would have had even in the snuggest of cottages.

We also discovered carefully preserved garments of long-ago fashions. While some of the gaudy costumes sent people into giggles and smirks, most of the fabrics—having been of the highest quality—remained in good condition. So many of the villagers had fled in their nightclothes from the cannon barrage that they stood in grave need of warmer garments. Best were trunks of liveries and house dresses that had been packed away when

Mother had chosen more modern ones. The women and children had a marvelous time sorting out and trying on the apparel.

The sight of Mistress Cooper enveloped in yards of a gauzy material had us all in tears of laughter, especially when she tried to essay a court courtesy and fell flat with an *oof* that also split the back of the dress. She was so distressed that it took Mother nearly half an hour to reassure her. Finally, Mother took a piece of fragile gauze in both hands and, with only the least pressure, split it easily.

"It must be well over a hundred years old, Mistress Cooper. Even the best of fabrics will deteriorate in that long a time."

"A hundred years, milady?" Mistress Cooper's distress was replaced by astonishment.

One chest was stuffed with the voluminous petticoats of the last century which could be turned into night-clothes. Another was full of men's shirts and knee britches. Fortunately many were made of good heavy cloth, and it was decided they could be lengthened against the wintry weather.

"And, I think," Mother said as people departed to their various sleeping chambers, "tomorrow we will see how to alter the old liveries and maids' dresses to fit. Unless there are other calls upon our time and effort."

There were not, though feeding and clothing one hundred and eighty-five homeless people required considerable organization and patience the next day. Mistress Cooper was up almost before Livvy, and the pair wakened four more women to start bread. Livvy did insist on reclaiming her largest cauldron to the kitchen after its night on the ramparts with oil, no longer boiling or needed. She remarked on the depth of the frost on the roofs and had a narrow escape falling into one of the gutters, but there had to be sufficient porridge and she would have braved much worse than mere frost to do her duty as Mallafret's cook. That report of the bitter cold worried Mother. Not that the Shupp had ever frozen solid, since it ran so swiftly. All was snug inside Mallafret Hall and Mother had to be content that she had accomplished that much.

Stuffed with hot porridge and tightly bundled with scarves and heavy capes of yesteryear's fashions, Andras and Achill led the older lads out to bring in more wood to replenish the fires which had to be kept burning. Even gloves were found in one wide storage drawer—though they were of such fine leathers that I saw Mother blanch as she handed them out—but cold fingers could fumble and this was no time to try to preserve the antiquated when present need was greater. Mind you, I had to go call the boys in when they were suspiciously long at a task that should have been completed more quickly. At that, Andras and Achill admitted that they had been first tempted to skate on the pathways—which were hoar-frosted and made excellent slides.

We spent the rest of the day inspecting the wealth within the trunks and presses under the eaves. Mother did return several of the more magnificent ball gowns to the cambric in which they had been swathed. The formal court wear, stockings, knee britches and such like were also set aside. The rest of the garments—the full sleeved fine cambric and muslin shirts, the long-skirted jerkins and vests, broadcloth jackets which could be dyed more suitable shades than buttercup yellow or pale green, blue, lavender and gray, and such breeches as there were of the durable fabrics—came out at once.

Every ground floor room became drapers' shops. Garments festooned tables, chairs, firescreens or waited in orderly piles. Such needles, threads and scissors as we possessed were kept busy until late that night, and it was nothing short of amazing how many people were clad in more modern fashion the next morning.

The intense cold continued. I heard it murmured often that some good had come out of the bombardment, for never would they have been so warm and comfortable in the homes they had lost.

Tray and Keffine returned midmorning for more supplies. They were red-cheeked and merry with their new responsibilities, but both had somehow cleaned up their garments and washed their faces. Keffine was mounted on a sturdy well-bred cob while Tray still rode the pony. Old as the venerable fellow was he too seemed to find his new occupation to his liking for he pranced and danced on his hindquarters as much as the cob did.

"We've some good news for the cottagers, Mother,"

43

Tray said, once again putting down his feet and letting the pony walk out from under him. Keffine's merry glance caught mine and I coughed into my hand rather than laugh outright. "You may laugh, Tirza," my brother said with such sublime arrogance that Mother and I both dissolved into gales of laughter.

"Thank you," I said, when I had quite exhausted myself with hilarity. "Bread's baked and some pies are ready and will only need to be reheated," I said, retreating into the house to assemble the victuals.

It was when I returned with my helpers, dressed in their new finery, that Tracell and Keffine Hyland gawked with surprise.

"Have you a troop of mummers, too?" Tray asked, though he accepted the baskets of food readily enough. In fact, he had the pony so laden that there was no room left for him to sit on the sturdy back. Keffine, likewise, dismounted because it was far more important that the food reach the hungry recipients than that he rode comfortably.

I glanced at our unusually clad assistants. "We have

been able to do what we could to clothe them all decently," I replied, "by turning out all those old trunks in the attic."

"What a splendid idea," Tray agreed, winking at me for the times we had played with the contents of those self-same discards. "Some came in little more than their shifts, shawls and clogs on their feet."

"Save some shirts and vests for us, would you?" Tray said, regarding his torn and battered raiment.

"You might tell the villagers that we have found quite a few things that survived the fires," Keffine said. He had the merriest blue eyes.

"Which is why you both look as if you'd been sifting through ash and dirt. Well done, well done," my mother said.

"One way of keeping warm," Tray remarked diffidently.

"But kindly thought of," Mother said.

"There's more usable than we'd've thought," Keffine said, accepting the basket of breads. "Though we did have a spot of trouble when an Effestrian patrol ventured to the riverbank and tried to interrupt our labors. We sent them off with such a rain of arrows, they fell over themselves running away."

"More slipping and sliding down the bank," Tray added, grinning.

Mistress Cooper and Mistress Chandler arrived just then, their arms full of cloaks.

"You will need these," Mother said, draping a cloak across Tray's shoulders.

Astonished, he held a fold up, almost sputtering with indignation. "Why, this has to have been last worn by great-great uncle . . ."

"Never you mind who wore it last, Viscount Mallafret," my mother said firmly. "It will doubtless deflect arrows as well as keep you warm."

Keffine Hyland bent his knees to allow Mistress Cooper to bestow one on his broad shoulders. He looked quite elegant.

The rest of the warm garments were carefully draped across cob and pony.

"They are indeed welcome, milady," Keffine said, bowing gratefully.

"And these will undoubtedly be as welcome while they hold together." Mother passed each a pair of heavy mailed gauntlets, so ancient that the cloaks were almost modern in comparison.

"Now, these are more suitable for warriors like us," Tray said, stuffing the gloved fingers as far down as he could force them. Then they made their way, proud and tall, down the avenue, leading the laden animals. I wasn't certain in my mind who looked more elegant, my brother or Keffine.

The bitter cold lasted a full week, so that Andras, Achill and some of the sturdier lads had to take cross saws and axes into the home woods to keep us supplied with firing. Under Mother's command, we took the oxen and the heaviest wain left in the village tithe-barn and brought back more wheat which had to be hand-ground, as the millwheel was frozen solid in the weir. Several of the men came back from the village and, with our gamekeeper and Tray to guide them, brought back deer and cleared the snares of whatever had been trapped and frozen to death.

While the worst of the cold held, we did not fear renewed attacks from the Effestrians, and Lord Monteros sent messengers to Mother, and from us to Princestown, that he had reinforced the riverbanks of his province to prevent enemy incursions. The returning courier brought very welcome letters from all our brave soldiers so we spent Solstice in a merriment that was far from the doleful occasion it might have been.

Not as bitter but still cold, the winter remained. On such fair days as there were, new dwellings began to rise in the village, replacing those burned to the ground. As Tray had said, iron pots and pans, skillets, even some crockery had survived the fire. And the chimneys.

Mallafret, in its turn, provided occupation for all to replace what was lost. Mother turned everything out of the attic spaces: chests, presses, tables (that might lack a leg or a brace), chairs that needed rerushing or regluing. She organized those handy with tools to make up additional stools or tables and arranged for the skilled carpenters to replace the lost dower chests. Mallafret was a hive of activity.

Rather than lose valuable space by setting up the big looms, Mother devised a clever and easier method of replacing bedding. In the course of refitting old-fashioned clothing to modern bodies, many pieces and hems and oddments had been cut off. These Mother gave to the youngest and oldest women to piece together into wide bedspreads. Then she had some of this year's wool crop carded fine and stitched in place on one side, while a backing was firmly stitched to provide a triple thickness. Some of the defter needlewomen, having finished redesigning clothing, made interesting patterns of the available colors so that some of the patchwork was quite beautiful as well as warm. All were delighted with the illustrious future use of what might have been discarded as rags.

Spring was late in coming that year, as if even the weather was at war with us. Fair days found everyone who could do anything, even if only holding a ladder steady, helping to rebuild the cottages. The fields were too wet or still too deeply frozen to be ploughed.

Everyone worried about planting and so complained to Mother.

"Well, I shall just have to see what can be done," Mother said and, putting on her oldest boots, mounted Courier, whose stately walk was slow. The best that Tray could say about him was that he eventually got where he was going. And he was very comfortable to ride.

Several times on Mother's tour, he became mired down and had to be hauled out of the mud. Mother spent several days out, going from farm to farm. Pausing in the village on her way, she noted the rise of new habitations. That cheered her, I know, because to have so many people about us constantly in Mallafret had lost any charm. The earlier comradeship in disaster had altered to squabbles that Mother had to arbitrate time and again, taking her away from more urgent planning.

After her inspection tour, she called all together: farmer and villager.

"Where there is too much water, we must dig little channels for it to run to the edges of the fields. Perhaps even line some depressions with stones to preserve the water should we need it in the summer. If this winter has been so wet, we may very well have a very dry summer."

So sensible was the suggestion that despite the very hard work to implement her scheme, it was accomplished. If not all of a field could be ploughed, enough was drained so that seed would not rot. Once such planting was done, work turned back to rebuilding the cottages. And in this regard, Mother had a great deal to say to improve the interiors, the major improvement being her insistence that local slate be used for the roofs rather than the traditional thatch. Since Bart the Thatcher's house had also burned, he allowed as how he could accept the change. By raising all the roofs by two feet, there was sufficient loft space under the eaves to provide more sleeping space and, for those on the ground level, considerably more privacy.

The inn was reconstructed next, with kitchens and nooks snug and open before the next story was completed. There were not yet many travelers but often couriers passed, and they were grateful for a full night's rest. Mother, in grave conversation with Matt the Innkeeper and his wife, decided that, all things considered, it wouldn't be a bad idea to have a large room added to one side of the Inn, suitable for village meetings, assemblies, Solstice dances, and any other functions that required a large indoor space.

"It will, of course," my mother said in the mild way she sometimes used to such good effect when trying to get her way, "be grand for our Victory Celebrations."

And so she had all the enthusiastic help such a project required. However, the large room first saw use as a hospice as walking wounded began to make their way to distant homes. They were grateful for the food and shelter at Mallafret Village, and Mother supervised such nursing as their injuries required.

"Those of Mallafret will have snug dwelling houses to come home to, thanks to your efforts, milady," Sir Minshall reminded her, seeing how downcast the injuries had made her who had been so cheerful through all our adversities.

"I'll have to see what I can do," she said, shaking her head and caressing the crystals.

All too soon, my own crystal would be placed on its chain about my neck, but the prospects of having a horse for my twin diminished from unlikely to impossible. We saw horses from far to the south being driven along the main road to Princestown, resupply for the cavalry.

"There's not one of them," Tray said, his scathing tone hiding disappointment, "worth bothering with. They all have four legs, a head and tail and that's the best that can be said."

Mother and I exchanged glances, and she sighed.

"Then it's as well we have no silver or gold to beg for one," Mother replied with a sly glance at him.

"A waste even if we had any!" Tray replied contemptuously. "They're not worth even stealing."

Taking a deep breath, he turned away from us and went off to help Siggie weed the vegetables.

Mother and I exchanged glances: hers nearly as doting as mine since we knew how keenly he was trying to hide an almost palpable frustration.

"I really will have to see what can be done."

"Mother," I said from all the wisdom of my nearly sixteen years, "sometimes even you can't provide the impossible. Besides which, he has set his heart on a Cirgassian, like our Courier . . . only not wind-broken."

With the slightest of smiles on her face and her long, slender, workworn fingers sliding up and down the dangling crystals, she replied, "It is true that the impossible takes longer, but the improbable is a force to be reckoned with."

The summer brought so little rain that those reservoirs which Mother had had us construct to drain or retain the excess winter water proved to be the salvation of what crops we had been able to nurture. As fortunate was the fact that Prince Sundimin, with our father now one of his most valued generals, was pursuing the war well into Effestrian lands. Our village was asked to send reinforcements of any male who had reached the age of sixteen and those over forty who were still able in body. This reduced our work force further and worried my mother more. For, inexorably, our sixteenth birthday neared and she feared that Tracell would have to answer the next draft. However much we had both longed to be sixteen and considered adult, that status had lost much of its long-desired charm.

Although it was the custom in our land that if a male child becomes adult at sixteen, it was also true that a girl of that age may put up her hair and go to balls and other social occasions. I, who had once dreamed all sorts of enchantments to occur during my first ball, drearily realized that no such festivity was likely. Imagine then my astonishment when Mother, all smiles and gladness, informed us that of course Mallafret Hall would celebrate our birthday with the traditional ball.

"And what, dear Mother, shall we have to wear to a ball?" I asked rather tartly, since Tracell and I were then most practicably attired in the sturdy knee breeches that even women were wearing as more durable apparel for hoeing fields and rebuilding cottages. Even the thought of a ball, however, was able to reawaken yearnings, which I had so firmly excluded from consideration.

"Why, my dears," and Mother's smile was so mischievous that I found myself smiling back, "we will have our choice of what we want to wear to a ball. A costume ball. You can't have forgotten all the lovely gowns, long coats, embroidered vests, and fine silken breeches which we so admired last winter after the village burned? Who will care if we dress in old-fashioned finery? But dress we will. And Livvy says there will be enough eggs and flour and sweetening to provide a proper birthday cake and other confections to make the occasion all that it should be. Your father put down wines at your births and these need only to be brought up from the cellar."

"But—but—" Even Tracell was now so accustomed to mundane substitutes that the thought of such extravagance startled him. Or maybe it was the thought of his long-desired and unattainable birthday horse!

"We may be short of many things, my dear Tray, but there are certain times when ceremony must be celebrated. And you both," she encircled our waists with her arms, "deserve whatever we can contrive. And I know exactly what I can do."

"Well, I can't say that you don't contrive minor miracles regularly, Mother," Tray said, admiringly. "But must I wear knee breeches?"

"Indeed you must, my love," she said, undeterred by his protest, "for you've as fine a leg as your father."

Hands raised in passionate rebellion, Tray took a deep breath.

"Not another word," my mother said, putting her fingers on his mouth. "You'll be surprised at how courtly you will appear. Every girl in the county will be eager to dance with you."

"No powder in my hair . . ." Tray said, waggling a finger under her nose.

"With such lovely titian locks as you have, of course not," Mother said, pretending outrage at the mere suggestion.

"And how are you going to get everyone else to dress up that way?" Tray demanded. I knew he did not wish to dress in uncommon fashion.

"We have not been the only family in the county to have seen what our ancestors put up in their attics," was Mother's blithe reply. "I think the pale green for you, Tracell, so I will allow some of the others to be loaned where they will fit."

By the time he had been forced to try on the pale green, with its heavy embroidery of silver and froth of lace (bleached to its original white and mildly starched), he spent quite a while observing himself in Mother's triple mirror. Shoes, with buckles and green heels, had also been found and fitted well enough.

"So gallant, milord," Mother said, and we both sank

into court curtsies that sent him into guffaws since we were still in our everyday breeches. (They were just a little ludicrous since they were much too long for us and reached our ankles.)

But the prospect had put him in a very good mood. Which, I think, was what Mother had in mind.

The entire village joined to help Mallafret Hall produce an evening that would be memorable. If the journals of our ancestors—which took up several shelves in the library—annotated in precise detail the lavish decorations and extravagant excesses of previous sixteenth birthdays, Mother decreed yet another sensible innovation. This Ball would start early enough in the evening so that the summer length of daylight would not require the use of the thousands of expensive and totally unobtainable tapers to fill the chandeliers and light the proceedings. Indeed, the dancing would be on the greensward below the terrace on the South Face of Mallafret Hall. The lawn, or so Andras and Achill vehemently declared, had been rolled and rolled and all but manicured with embroidery scissors to a level that would be as smooth a surface for dancing as any parquet floor. Garlands of honeysuckle from the hedgerows, gathered by the villagers, draped across the terrace balustrade and wherever such floral decorations were needed. Everyone seemed determined to make this a truly momentous occasion. We were not even daunted by the sultry weather that augured of possible thundershowers. Indeed, from time to time, I could have sworn I heard distant thunder in the east. If that were the case, since our weather went from west to east, our evening would not be spoiled.

Barbecue pits were dug for the several oxen (who might be tough to eat due to their extreme age, but they wouldn't have survived another winter anyway). Many braces of pheasant, grouse, chicken, pigeon, dove, and goose were turning on spits. Carp, tench, and the other fish that had been taken by diligent anglers from local streams were ready to be grilled. The odors of roasting meats and game encouraged us to work the harder to make all ready for the party.

"We all deserve it," Diana said, and Desma, much as I had been the silent second to my brother's remarks, nodded emphatically.

"Now you must sit still," Catron told them, for we had

dressed them first since our toilettes would take longer. As a special concession to keep them occupied, they were allowed to watch us dress, Catron giggling nearly as much as I, as we struggled into the corselettes and hoops and petticoats required to underpin our lovely gowns. And then they took turns pulling the corset strings in so tight I was afraid I'd never be able to dance, much less eat of our birthday feast.

Mother had designated the pale yellow gown which had been so admired the previous winter for Catron, since it suited not only her fourteen years but her dark hair and fair skin. As Catron was taller than whomever the dress had been created for, it reached the middle of her lower limbs, the perfect length for her. Since I was now a few hours short of being officially sixteen, I was allowed to wear a much more elaborate and delectable confection of white gauze over silver silk. Throwing a muslin cape over Catron's shoulders, Mother first braided my sister's dark locks tightly to a point just below the nape of her neck. Then she allowed the lovely natural curls to fall to Catron's waist: still a young style but with just enough fashion to please my sister.

My dark red hair was piled and pinned atop my head, save for the three long ringlets which, with her curling iron, Mother created to fall from the back knot of my hair across my shoulder to hang nearly to the décolletage of the low cut gown.

Then she placed on both our heads, as if tiaras of price-less gems, headbands of honeysuckle and daisies. Catron and I exclaimed and twirled and whirled in front of the mirror while our younger sisters were struck dumb at the change in us.

"These should be roses or something more exot-ic," Mother said apologetically as she arranged gar-lands. "Now, for just one more detail," she said and left the room.

We were both fidgeting at what seemed a very long delay—we were so eager to show everyone else how fine we looked—when she returned with two flat black velvet cases: one round, one long.

"Pearls are suitable for you, Catron," she said and opened the first of the cases to remove the strand of pink-toned pearls that fit around Catron's lovely neck as if they had been strung for her alone. "Now, you may take your sisters downstairs and you are *all*," and Mother held up a stern finger, "to sit quietly in the hall where you may move *only* to welcome early-come guests should some arrive before Tracell, Tirza and I descend."

An ecstatic Catron let go of her pearls to take her sisters' hands and leave the room.

Then, with an air of ceremony, Mother turned to me, the long case in her hand.

"You are not precisely sixteen, dearest Tirza, but you have acted with such wisdom in the last trying years that I feel I am conforming to tradition in letting you choose your crystal today, on the eve of your sixteenth birthday."

I almost burst into tears. "But what shall we do about Tray and his horse, mother?"

Tears were in her eyes as she embraced me.

"You make my heart leap with pride, my darling. Not that I haven't cudgeled my brains in an effort to make his birthday wish come true, but . . ." and she gave a little sigh, half-sob, half a catch of her breath. Brisk again, she opened the case to show me the four crystals nestled there, each on fine linked chains similar to those she wore: one crystal for each of her daughters. "I will tell

62

you—when we have more time—how to understand the use of these crystals. You will find that their main purpose is an aid to help you focus your mind on what needs to be done. I believe yours will help you refine instincts that I have already seen you exhibit."

I didn't really absorb her words, for the sight of beautiful jewels awed me. I fancied I heard gentle music, the kind heard when delicate crystal is lightly pinged by a finger. No two of the crystals in that box were alike. One, two finger-joints long, was the palest of blues, its facets cut cleanly and ending in a point. Another, slightly shorter, blushed the pink of the most delicate rose. The third was the dainty yellow-green of the peridot.

"That's Catron's," I blurted out.

Mother chuckled. "You may well be right, my love."

It was the fourth, the clear one, not white but seeming to hold all the rainbow colors when the sun coming through the window touched it briefly. It was the one to which my hand instinctively went. I saw out of the corner of my eye that Mother nodded once, as if she had known this would be my choice.

"This was the one you reached for when you were

barely three months old and my mother and grand-mother brought crystals to see which would suit you best."

"That long ago?"

"As the world turns, it is not *that* long ago, love."

She put it around my neck and embraced me with a kiss on each cheek and one on my lips. As soon as the crystal settled against the skin of my chest, I could feel the warmth of it.

"Oh!" I was surprised.

"Oh?" Mother echoed, her eyebrows rising in query.

"It's warm. I thought a crystal would be cool."

My mother gave me a long and searching look. "That depends on the crystal, but obviously your choice is well made and the crystal is content to be worn by you." We were both startled by the sound of thunder. "It seems the heavens agree with me. When we have more time, I will explain some of the properties of these particular crystals and how the women of our line have learned to depend on them."

"Do they," and I pointed to the three she wore—this

time looped onto a black velvet band at her throat so that each, the tender-blue, then the white and the deep green—dangled separately, "tell you what to do all the time, Mother?"

She laughed. "Not in so many words, love, but they do help focus the mind when sensible thought is required. Generally they take some heat from our bodies. If it should ever get very hot or very cold, come to me instantly. Now," and she turned brisk, "you must help me dress, for if I do not mistake the sounds, some of our guests are arriving."

Indeed, the rumbling thunder to the east had caused many of our invited guests to hurry, lest they in their finery be caught in a sudden shower. Mind you, the manner of transport which brought many of them started the party in high good humor. So few horses remained in the county that other animals had been substituted. Several carts were drawn by not so willing pairs of goats. One elegant barouche was stately drawn by two sets of yoked oxen, while four mismatched mules pulled a landau. More than one conveyance used donkeys, hee-hawing up the drive as if commenting on their new occupation so that all would notice their promotion. Several farmers actually pushed their elegantly dressed wives in barrows so their dainty fabrics would not be soiled by road dust. Those from the village were perhaps grateful that they did not have far to walk. I did see some reach the gates and pause to dust their feet before putting on their dancing slippers.

Of course, Mother had been very generous with the contents of our attic. We did recognize some of the fine gowns and male attire. And if the fashions were of different centuries, we were all most elegantly costumed. Tracell had never looked so handsome, nor so like Father, as he did in the pale green wide-skirted long jacket, with the beautifully embroidered paler green waistcoat and white silk knee breeches. I felt that Keffine was as handsome in the blue, and his father, Lord Hyland, posed as a remarkable figure in his purple. Lady Hyland was certainly flattered by the lavender silk with its gauzy overskirt trimmed with silver lace. There had not been enough of the old-fashioned apparel to fit or costume everyone of rank in the county from our stores, but following our example, many appeared in what they had been able to discover. The gentlemen attired themselves, if informally, in fine cambric white full sleeved shirts, worn with elegant lacy froths at the throat, long vests, and tight court pants. Women appeared in every sort of bodices, full skirts, and embroidered or lacy aprons every bit as elegant as their menfolk. As well we were out of doors, for many had preserved their garments from the moth by camphor, which airing had not completely removed and which the heat of the afternoon made more redolent.

Old liveries had been unearthed and freshened so that those who served the gathering did so as stylishly as those they waited upon. I don't know who found the outfits for the village musicians, but they were certainly clad for a grand occasion and seemed indefatigable in their energetic playing of old galliards, gavottes, reels, set dances and minuets. Their tankards were rarely left unreplenished. Perhaps the food did not rival the victuals or fancies that had been served at other such Balls, but there was sufficient for all to partake until the roasts were finished. Portions of the fish and fowl were passed around, with napkins, and with fine wine or beer or cider to wash these tidbits down, so the dancing took on an exuberance that equaled the occasion.

By tradition, the birthday child or children danced first. It should have been my father who bowed to ask for my hand, but Tracell did the honors for me. And to accept his hand I had to release my beautiful, exciting crystal for the first time since Mother had put it on my neck. Maybe, just maybe, my fervent prayers for him would be answered, though I had not been able to focus my mind on any manner in which I could spring a horse out of nowhere for Tray. Then Tray, again assuming my father's traditional role, swirled Mother, ravishing in the deep red that was so close a match to her glorious hair, onto the floor while the spectators cheered.

Keffine was next to ask my hand for a dance, and I only too delighted to accede as Tray partnered an ecstatic Catron. As my white and silver skirts whirled against Keffine's blue coat, I felt we made as handsome a couple as Mother and Tray. Keffine had to relinquish my hand to his father who, while no longer as agile as his son, had obviously instructed Keffine in all manner of dances. Protocol now properly observed, others took the floor.

During the short intervals, we were aware of more thunder, but no one was going to permit mere weather to interrupt this party. Who knew when the young men asking to dance with me or Catron (since Mother permitted her to stand up for the reels and sets) or those of the other pretty girls of our neighborhood would spend their next days? So many were now eligible to answer any new muster that the prince might call. I won't say that the atmosphere had even a touch of frenzy or premonition, though my crystal continued to feel comfortably warm against my skin, but this evening was for our enjoyment. And we were all determined to forget such things as the war and the sparse harvest that must see us through another long winter with so many other items in scarce supply.

We were indeed so single-minded in our enjoyment of the pleasures of the occasion that it wasn't until the horse walked out onto the terrace that we were forced to recall what we had managed to place at the back of our minds.

It was Andras who caught up the one remaining rein, and only half of it at that. The horse was so weary that it was possibly as happy to stand still. My first thought was that it was a Cirgassian, though nowhere near as exhausted as Courier had been on his arrival at Mallafret. The fiddlers stopped, bows scraping dissonantly, the flute piping awkwardly into silence and the accordion ending on a dissonance from lack of air. We all turned and stared.

This horse could not be the answer to *my* prayers, for dried blood and lather coated the creature. Its saddle was askew and the dark stain smeared on the seat could only be dried blood. No stirrups remained, nor a saber scabbard nor saddlebags.

Both Tray and Keffine approached the horse carefully, for the animal was in distress, its sides heaving. Tray caught a bun from the nearest plate, which he held out to the animal. It sniffed, extending its neck, snatched the bun, and devoured it. At a gesture from Tray, Andras and

Achill immediately filled their hands with bread to bring to Keffine and him. In that sudden silence, we were all aware that the thunder we had attributed to the weather had not been caused by that phenomenon, and fear spread as rapidly as if it had the night of the first bombardment we had suffered.

Because we were at the back of the house, on the greensward, with music enthusiastically played, the noise to the east had been muffled. Hand on my crystal, which was neither hot nor cold but as warm as my skin, I turned to Mother. She had her hand spread over the three at her neck and gave the littlest shake of her head.

"We had best investigate," Lord Hyland said and glanced hopefully at the horse.

"He's wounded, Lord Hyland," Tray said, pointing out the clotted blood down his near side, discoloring the white fetlock.

"The saddle's wet, Tray," Keffine said, "and with water. He's been swimming." As the horse continued to munch the food offered him, Keffine carefully loosed the girth of the off-center saddle and removed it from the horse's back. The badly placed saddle had rubbed raw patches.

Achill had the presence of mind to find a basin and fill it with water, which the horse sucked eagerly.

"Milord." One of the farmers came up to Lord Hyland with a big sturdy mule. "It's not at all what I'd offered in better times . . ."

"Ooh, not in those britches, milord," Lady Hyland exclaimed, appalled to see such splendor ruined in a saddle.

"Keffine, see what else there is to ride," Lord Hyland said and, disregarding his wife's continued reproaches, mounted the mule.

"I'll come, too," Tracell said, and encouraging the horse to follow, beckoned for his brothers to accompany him.

Donkeys were gathered from the paddocks in which they had been tethered. Mother and other ladies brought out the muskets, long rifles and such other weapons as might be useful, handing them around to the quickly assembled reconnoitering force. Then Tray trotted out from the stable yard on his pony, feet stuck out in his fine shoes so as not to be dragged on the ground. He had discarded his elegant coat and vest and somehow found a more practical pair of ancient trousers, which he had secured with a stirrup leather about his slim waist. Keffine, down to shirtsleeves and an equally disreputable pair of breeches, bestrode a donkey not much larger than Tray's venerable pony.

So variously mounted, the men sallied forth. Lord Hyland, on the much larger mule, led the way, equipped with the saber and pistols my mother had supplied.

Those who could not find four legs to use—no one attempted any of the goats—used their own two to follow Lord Hyland, leaving the rest of us in the midst of the party splendor.

I took such comfort as I could from the fact that my lovely crystal remained merely warm. I saw Mother's fingers alternating between her three and moved to her side. Once the men had gone, we women and children seemed directionless, all joy in our festivities abandoned.

"Well, we certainly cannot allow the roasts to burn," Mother said, taking charge again. "Mistress Cooper, will you not tend one, and Mistress Chandler, the other. Tirza love, gather up the aprons our chefs discarded. I for one do not care to ruin my finery. Livvy, Catron and Tess can see to the spits with whoever is willing to help turn them. We cannot waste good food, and doubtless the men will be hungry when they return."

"Shouldn't we change, Mother?" I asked.

My mother smiled. "No," she said slowly. "We must allow you as much of your birthday as possible."

"I've *had* my birthday, Mother," I said, for the first time contesting her.

That caused everyone to stop and stare at me and, for one moment, I could have sunk in the ground with dismay at my impudence.

"Thunder's gone," Mistress Cooper announced into the silence that lengthened as we all listened as hard as we could.

"It could have *been* thunder," Mistress Chandler offered.

"That horse was wounded," Lady Hyland said sternly. "With saber cuts. And he had swum the river. Clearly he escaped from some sort of a battle."

"The men will send a messenger as soon as may be to

reassure us. And do they all or only some return, there will be edible food to sustain them. So please to turn that ox before it becomes charcoal, Mistress Chandler." My mother spun one finger to remind the woman of her duty.

That was when three more horses were seen, gazing as if they had seen nary a blade of green grass for weeks. Two had no saddles and only torn remnants of bridles; the third was so badly scored on flank and withers that it was obvious the animal had followed its picket mates out of habit. They offered no resistance at all when we tried to lure them into the stable yard, where Siggie and those lads too young to be allowed to accompany the scouting party were able to attend them.

Mother found some sort of a driving coat, wearing it back to front, to cover her red dress because the most badly injured animal would need to have the terrible gash along his flank stitched or he would die from blood loss. I found a similar garment—one of father's I think— to protect my ball gown so I could sew up the gashes on the first animal, although Siggie had to use a twitch to keep him still enough for me to set the stitches. There were many willing helpers to wash and spread honey on the nicks and smaller cuts and generally see to the comfort of our four war refugees.

By the time we had finished those, just as Mother and I were about to doff the thick and confining garments, more horses stumbled in. . . . Cirgassians from their small pointed ears and conformation.

"My darling Tirza," Mother said to me, bemused as we watched a veritable troop of wet and tired animals limping into the yard—for horses will smell the presence of other equines as well as food. "I know how close you are to your twin, but surely you should have realized that I was going to make sure of some sort of a birthday horse for him?"

"Yes, but I wanted to make *certain sure*, Mother." My hand went to my crystal and I snatched it away, blowing on my fingers.

Mother, seeing that, reached for hers and, with equal alacrity, let them go.

"What is it, Mother?" I cried fearfully.

"Off with that garment," and she was stripping hers,

spreading her skirts out again from the confinement. "My hair? Is it mussed?"

"No, but our hands—"

While we had washed before tending the animals, we had not yet removed the traces of our ministrations.

Leaning over the horse trough in the stable yard without touching her dress to its wet sides, mother scrubbed her hands and arms as quickly as she could, gesturing for me to do so. We also heard shouting that added haste to our ablutions. She did pause long enough to be sure there was nothing under her fingernails, and I did the same. The cheers and shouts were jubilant, coming from the front of the Hall.

Mother picked up her skirts and ran, skipping around the droppings which no one had had time to sweep up from the usually spotless cobbles. I followed, also trying to straighten the edges of my overskirt that had been crushed down under the protective clothing I had worn. We also had to wend our way past even more horses that had run away from whatever battle they had ridden into.

We took the side gate out of the former rose garden

that had supplied us with vegetables the past two years and down the pebbled side of Mallafret. Mother's upraised arm stopped my helter-skelter progress, for the wide driveway was full of horses, mules, men and weeping women embracing haggard but happy soldiery. Lord Hyland sat his mule with great dignity and, seeing our arrival, pointed and shouted.

"Here they are, milord!"

Out of the press a horse was urged forward, and Mother, uttering a cry of great joy, ran in that direction. I started to follow but halted, taking in what she evidently ignored or, in relief at the sight of his tall figure, did not see: bandages and a tunic that showed tears and holes. My eyes fixed on the left hand, reaching for her, and the bandage that looked far too narrow to be covering four fingers. An even older, dirtier wrapping covered the left side of his head, half hidden under a military cap set at a jaunty angle as if to hide as much of the bandage as possible. But even as she reached him, she touched first his left hand and then his forehead. Then allowed herself to be swung up in his arms and twirled around.

I could see her speaking to him and knew, without any

sound, what she must be saying: "I must see what I can do about these."

Then Father threw back his head, laughing. "Why else do you think I have returned to you?" he said with such a jubilant tone that I knew he had not been as badly injured as he appeared. He whirled her again and, though one cheek was pressed against hers, I could see him wince. Well, he was home and Mother would certainly see what she could do about healing him.

From the fragments of joyful welcome around me, I knew that the war was over, that the thunder we had heard had come from Prince Sundimin's artillery, sending the Effestrians running for whatever safety they could find. Even their most recent allies, the plains' Cirgassians whose brave horses had taken refuge at Mallafret Hall, were in full retreat . . . many of them no doubt reduced to walking.

Father had been ordered south along the Shupp to intercept whatever stragglers came ashore to terrorize our people or seek merciful sanctuary from that final rout. (Not many that attempted the river survived.) The Shupp might not have been an insurmountable obstacle for horses bred to cross the swift and dangerous mountain rivers of the Cirgassian homelands, but only the strongest of human swimmers could have breasted those treacherous currents and come ashore. We learned later that many of the Cirgassian horses that managed to stagger up our banks had been swept miles down from their point of entry on the final battleground.

Then Father strode towards me, and I nearly sobbed to see the twinkling in his eyes, the way they crinkled with his happiness, and the proud expression on his dirty tired face: pride of me, his daughter.

"I did mean to be here at your sixteenth, daughter dear, but that is surely tomorrow unless I have somehow lost a day in that fearsome battle we won."

"We were informed that there would be another muster, my love," Mother said, one arm about his waist, heedless of the mud, dust and other stains now rubbing against her beautiful gown, so glad was she to be holding him again, "so it seemed a sensible idea to celebrate the day before should Tray be required to answer his prince's call."

"So you decided on a costume ball?"

"Indeed, my dear lord," Mother said, laughingly dismissing the past years of hardship and scarcities, "a costume ball was the very thing. And indeed the only festive apparel most of us had to our backs." She gestured to the guests, mingling now with restored husbands, fathers and sons. "And the early hour makes it unnecessary to use tapers, which we don't have anyway."

"We could not have had a more glorious welcome home had we sent out invitations, my love. How marvelous it is to see elegant women in beautiful gowns!" Then he leaned forward to touch the crystal at my throat. "As I recall, it is the very one your baby hands reached for." He kissed my forehead and then each cheek. "So where is my birthday son?" he now demanded, wheeling Mother around to search for Tracell in the throng. "What finery did he assume for this prenatal celebration? I have brought him something which I believed he greatly desired and which, indeed, I had promised to provide."

He pointed then to where his war-horse stood, single-mindedly cropping grass. That was when we realized his equerry held the reins of two grazing horses and was being pulled first in one direction and then the other. The unsaddled animal was nearly as tall as Father's and so dark a shade he gleamed bluely in the now fading evening light.

"Tracell is in a very elegant shade of green . . ." Mother began and then pointed down the avenue.

"Great heavens . . ." my father exclaimed, so stunned at the sight that he slapped his right hand to his forehead. For Tray, legs straight out before him, was galloping the pony across the lawn, the nimble little beast weaving his way among the assembled.

Father, roaring with laughter at the approaching vision, doubled up with mirth as Tray dropped his legs to the ground and let the pony run out from under him. "That will never do for the son of the General Lord Eircelly."

"I was setting sentries along the Shupp, Father, before your sergeant arrived to take over their disposition and informed me of your return," Tray said, standing just short of father, unsure whether to bow or salute. Father took the initiative and embraced his son—the two were nearly of a height so much had Tracell grown in the last two years. As men will, they were thumping each other on the back until both Mother and I saw that Tracell's young strength had too much force for a man who was certainly not recovered from his wounds.

Tracell caught Mother's gesture and stepped back from Father, a trifle embarrassed at how warm a greeting he had given a nation's hero.

"Bring the Cirgassian over here, Barton," my father called to his equerry. "My old fellow knows he's home and will not wander." So Barton, wrapping the charger's reins safely around his neck, trotted over with the fine young animal. "One of my spoils, Tray, when we took an entire remount contingent by surprise. I knew he would suit you. Rising three and entire. I doubt his like will be matched anywhere." Father beamed with pride as Tracell, his eyes gleaming with delight as he circled the proud horse who stood, head high, as if he knew he was being closely inspected. "Prince Sundimin himself approved my choice when he learned the reason for the gift."

Just then Andras, Achill and two of their peers came charging through the stable gate.

"There's ever so many more wandering in, Tray, that Siggie doesn't know where to put them . . . *Father!*"

The Cirgassian plunged in alarm at their ecstatic race to Father, and the two boys all but climbed him in their efforts to kiss and hug him joyfully. They had, indeed, been so busy succoring the tired and injured strays that they had not realized what had happened at the front of the Hall.

"Well, let us just see what other jetsam has landed in our demesne," my father said, setting the boys down again and letting himself be pulled towards the stable yard. He looked back to see that Tracell had calmed the excitable young horse and was leading him towards a quieter section of our crowded front lawn.

"My dear Talarrie," my father exclaimed as he paused to behold the stable yard so full of horses there seemed little space for the grooms attempting to feed and water them, "could it be that you have overworked your crystals?"

"I asked only for one," she said and pointedly did not glance in my direction, though I, too, had only asked for one. "But since we must replace horses for all our tenants and neighbors, perhaps that accounts for these numbers."

"You have always been the most generous of—" He broke off, stiffening, his head unerringly turning towards greensward where the delectable aromas of roasting meats quite overwhelmed the odors which can occur in any stable yard. "Is it at all possible that there might be something left of this early birthday feast?" he asked, his face wistfully hopeful.

She patted his hand and turned him in the right direction where I knew that our festivities would recommence with true joy and celebration.

"I'll see what we can do!"

As it was then, so it is now.